-To those who shine...

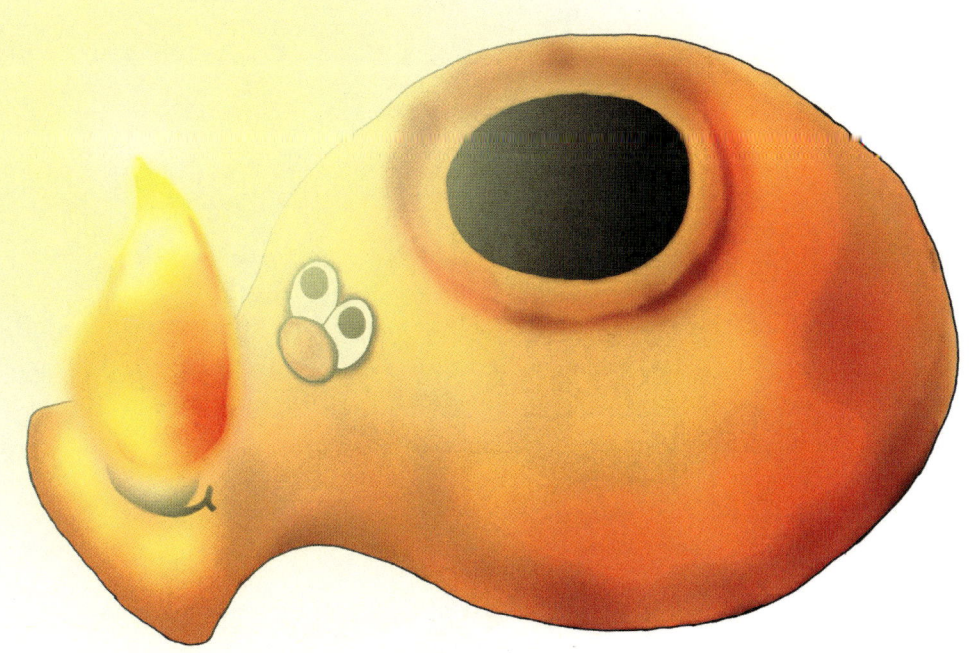

The Oil Lamp© 2024 by Dawn Stephens

All rights reserved. No part of this publication may be reproduced or transmitted in any form without the prior written permission of the publisher. Please send your requests to Dawn@dawnstephensbooks.com

Author: Stephens, Dawn
Layout and Design: Dawn Stephens
Editing: Crystal Bowman

LCCN: 2024917868
ISBN: 978-1-945975-93-6
Second Edition: 2024
First Published in 2020

1. Potters--Juvenile fiction.
2. Shine—Juvenile fiction.
3. Christian life--Juvenile fiction

Published by EA Books Publishing, a division of Living Parables of Central Florida, Inc. a 501c3

EABooksPublishing.com

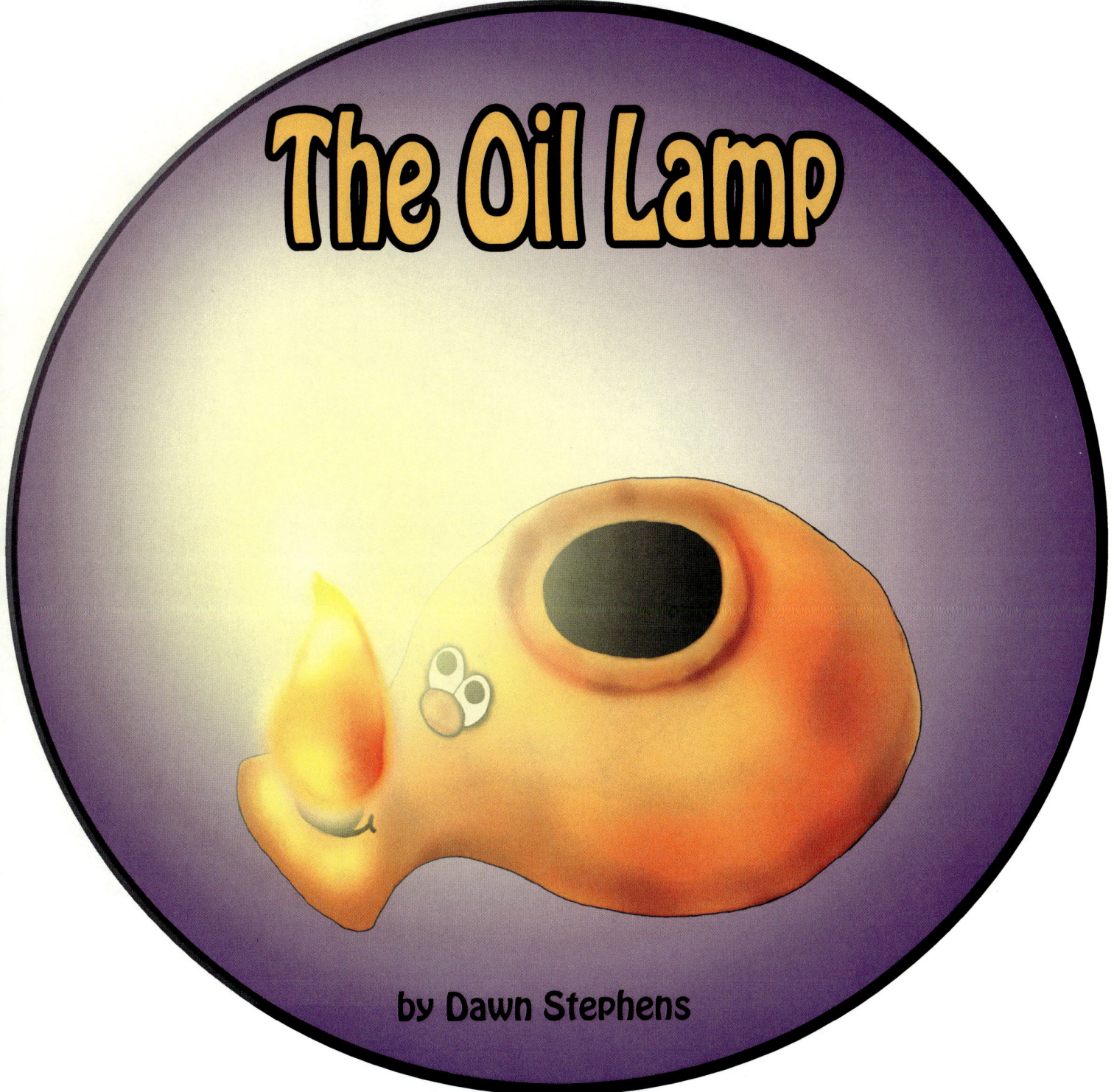

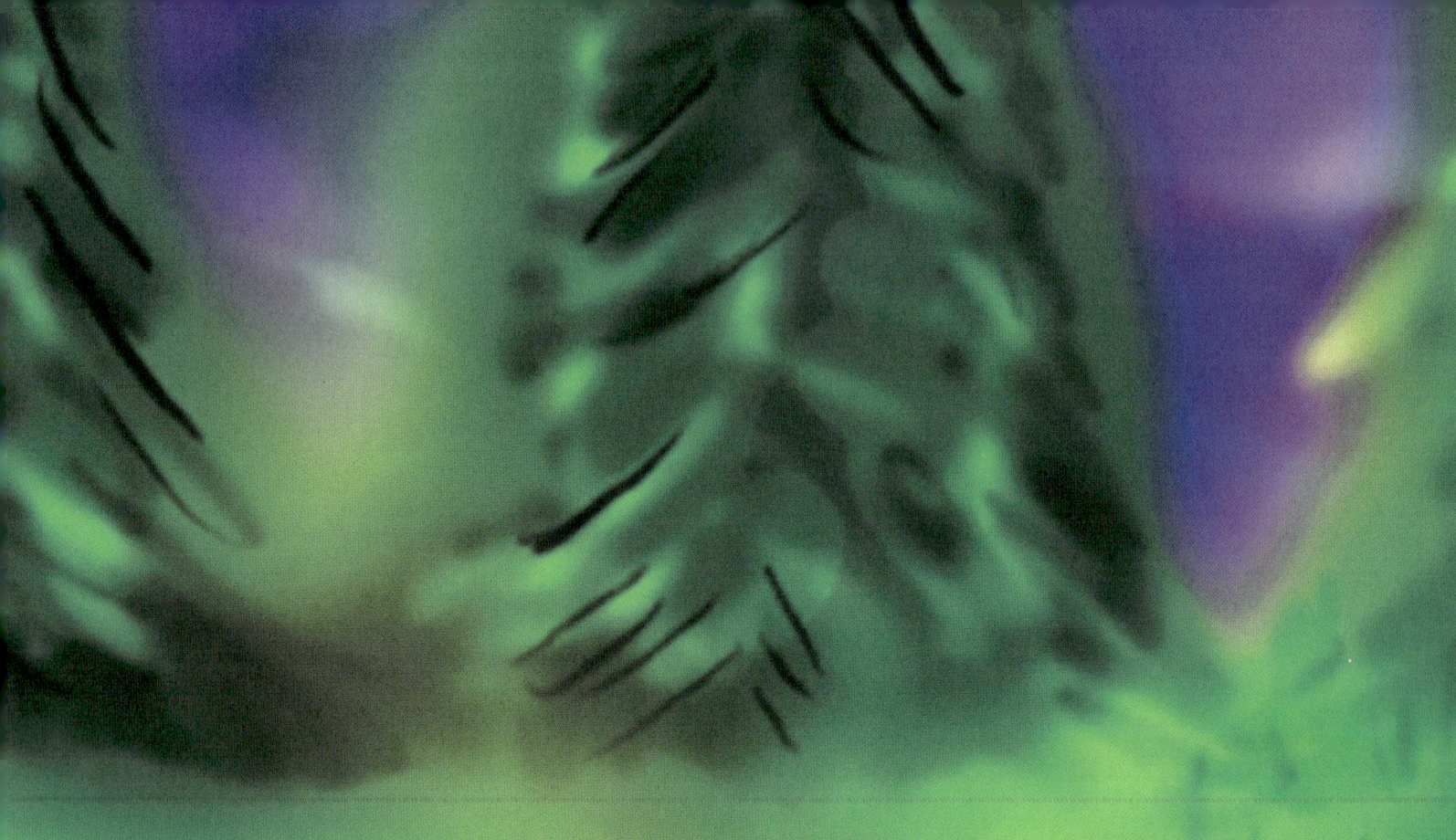

Everything was wonderful in the potter's workshop. A vessel named Little Pot grew fruit, while another vessel named Tea Pot brewed warm tea. They looked forward to giving their tea and fruit to the potter each day.

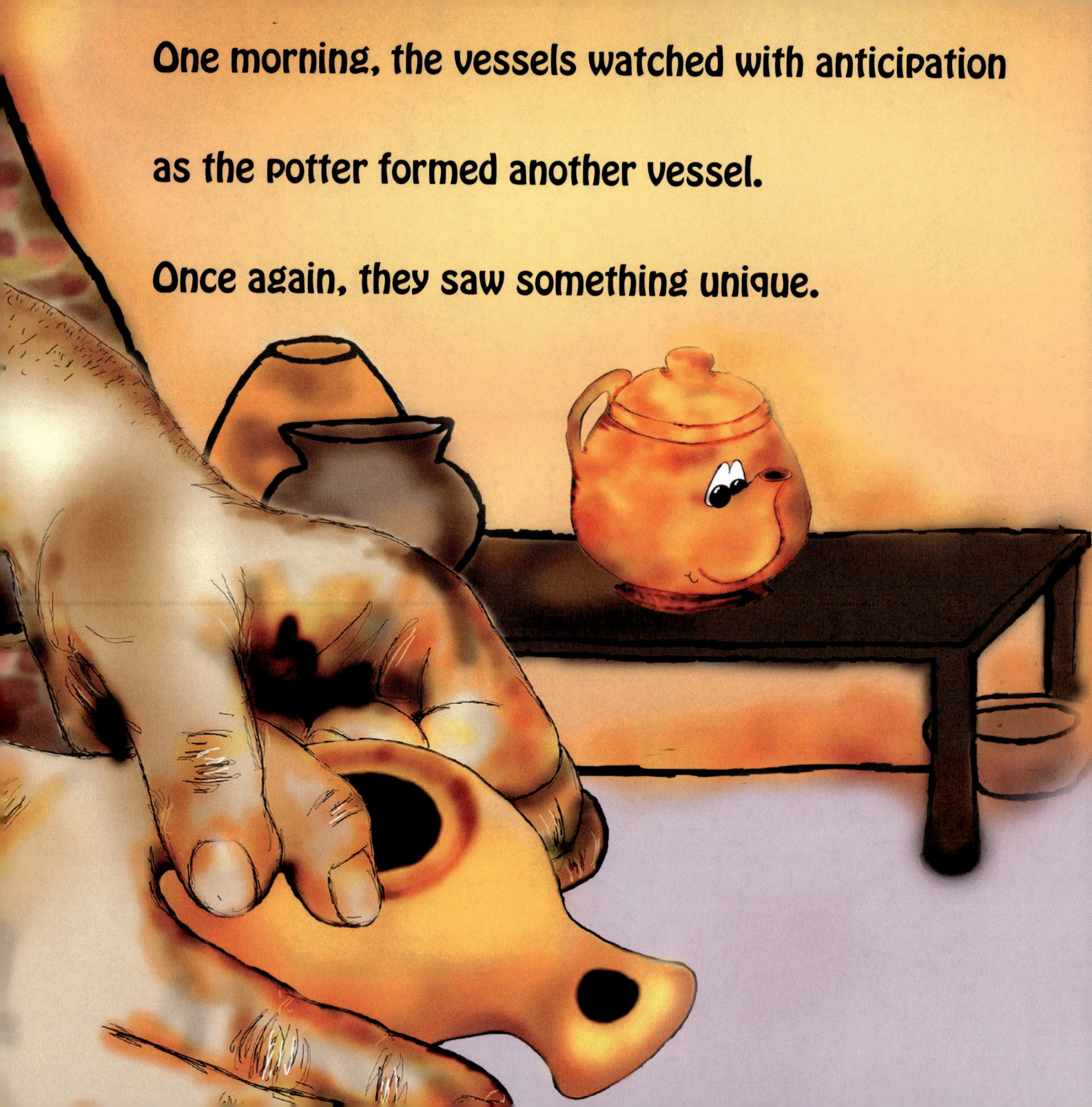

One morning, the vessels watched with anticipation as the potter formed another vessel.

Once again, they saw something unique.

The new vessel was round and flat.

It had two holes in the top. One was larger than the other, but both holes were small.

When the tiny vessel came out of the kiln, the potter placed a small rope called a wick inside the larger hole and pulled it out through the smaller hole. Then he filled it with beautiful, gold liquid and named it Oil Lamp.

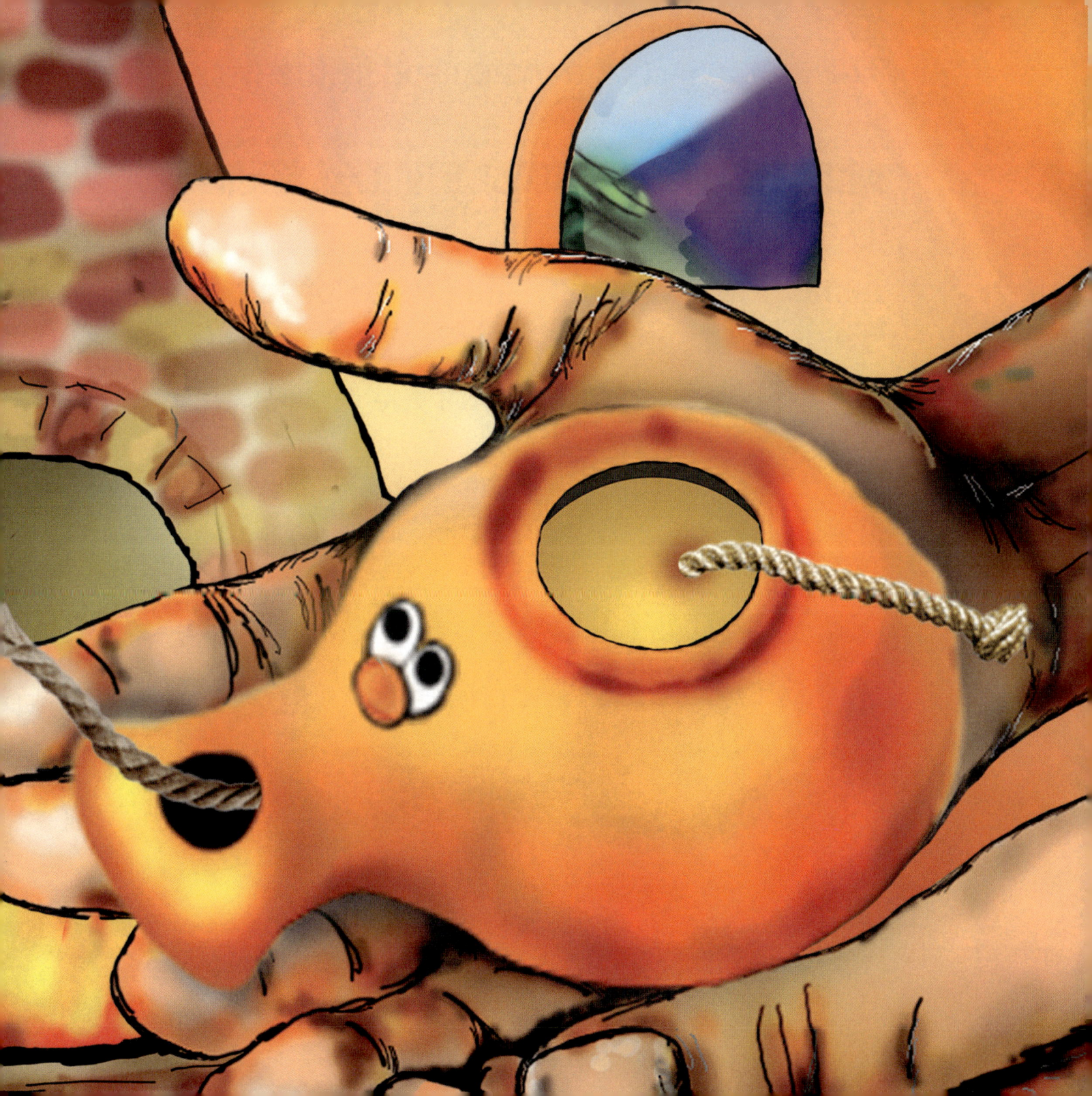

The potter struck a match and lit the wick with fire. Oil Lamp shook with fear at the flame it held. Tea Pot and Little Pot felt the warm glow of the lamp's light.

Afraid of the flame, Oil Lamp hid under a bowl, which caused the flame to go out.

The potter smiled and stayed to visit with Tea Pot and Little Pot. He poured himself some tea and ate a few berries.

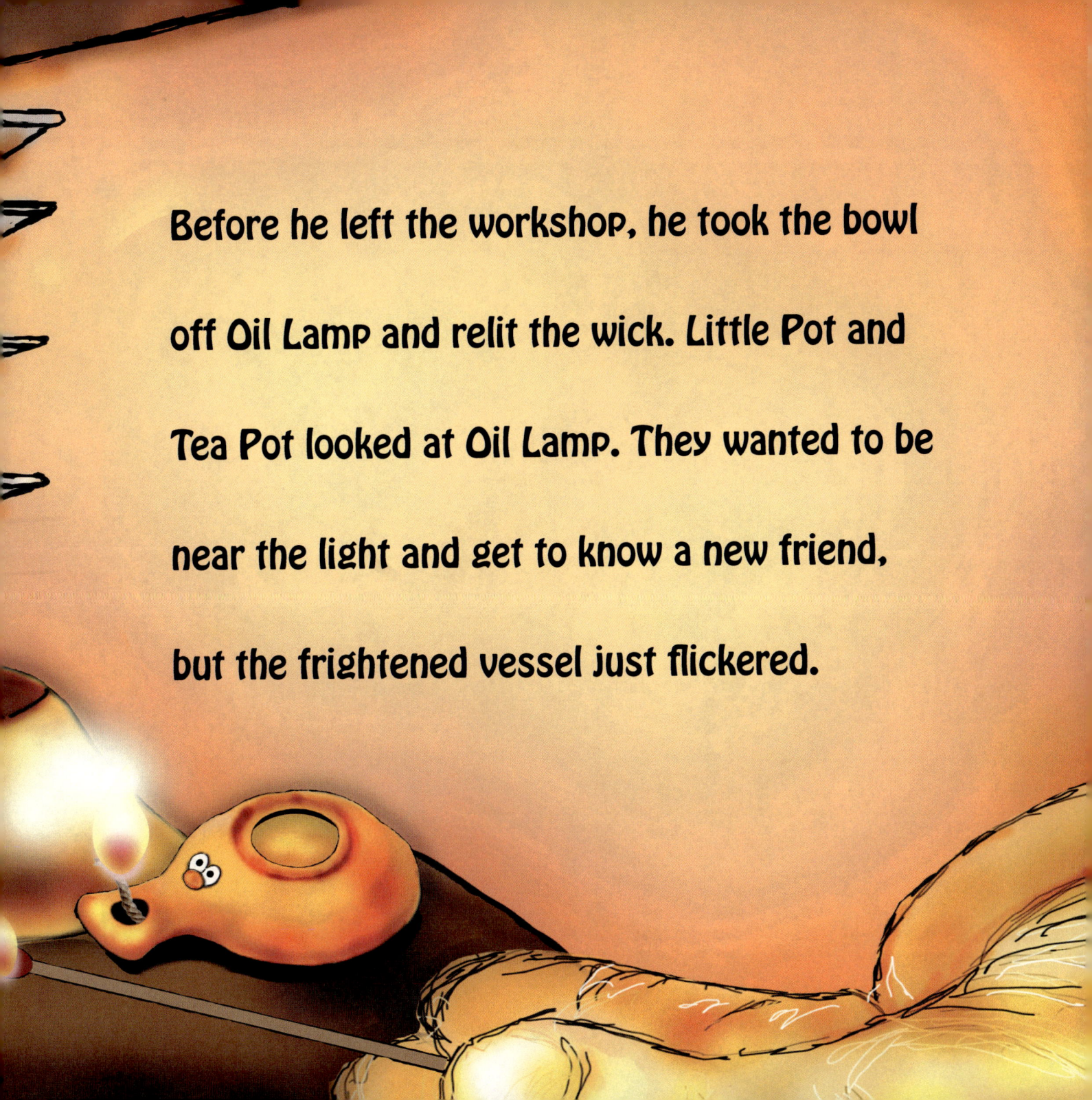

Before he left the workshop, he took the bowl off Oil Lamp and relit the wick. Little Pot and Tea Pot looked at Oil Lamp. They wanted to be near the light and get to know a new friend, but the frightened vessel just flickered.

That night, the sky grew dark, and the air turned cold.

A storm was coming. Oil Lamp's flame grew dimmer as it hid from the darkness.

Rain pelted the windows, and wind shook the workshop's walls.

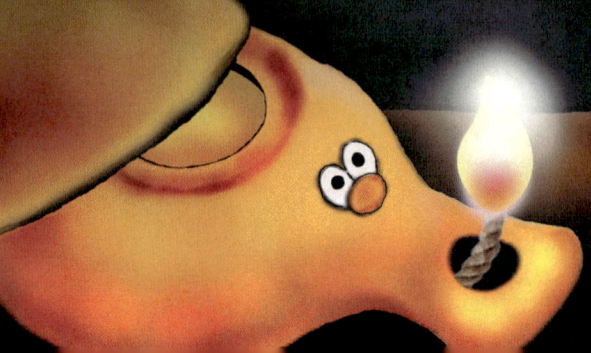

A flash of lightning made scary shadows appear,

followed by a loud, booming crash of thunder.

All the vessels on every shelf and in every

corner woke up with fear.

Soon, the vessels noticed the small glow shining from behind the bowl. It was Oil Lamp!

A steady flame was rising from the lamp and the warm light reminded them of the potter and the peace they felt in his presence. When Oil Lamp saw the vessels coming closer, it stopped being afraid and burned even brighter.

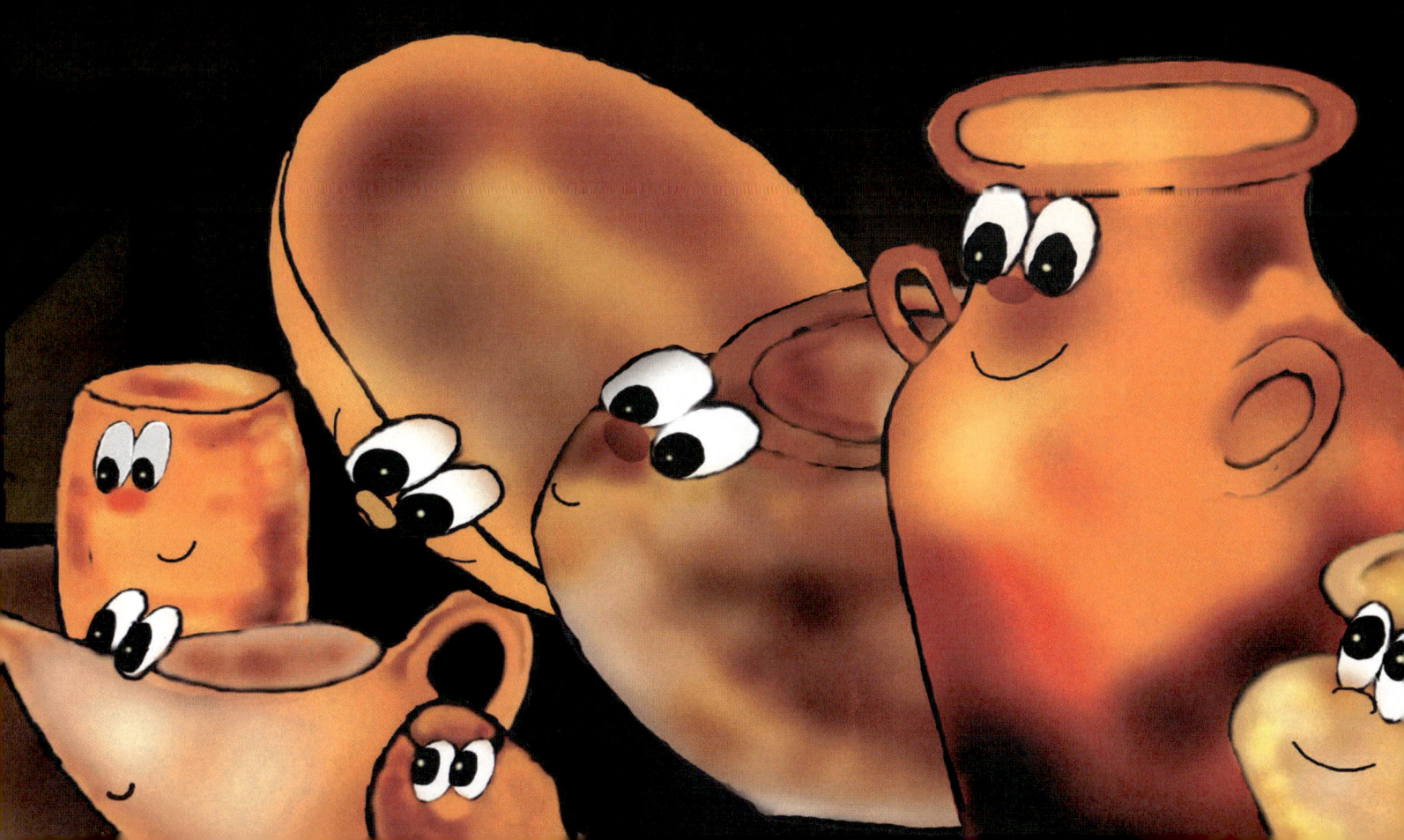

None of the other vessels carried a flame, and the fire made Oil Lamp feel bigger, stronger, and more important than the rest.

Oil Lamp stretched out the wick and burned proudly at the other vessels. The warm light made the vessels feel safe in the storm. But after a while Oil Lamp's flame got too big. The vessels felt burned.

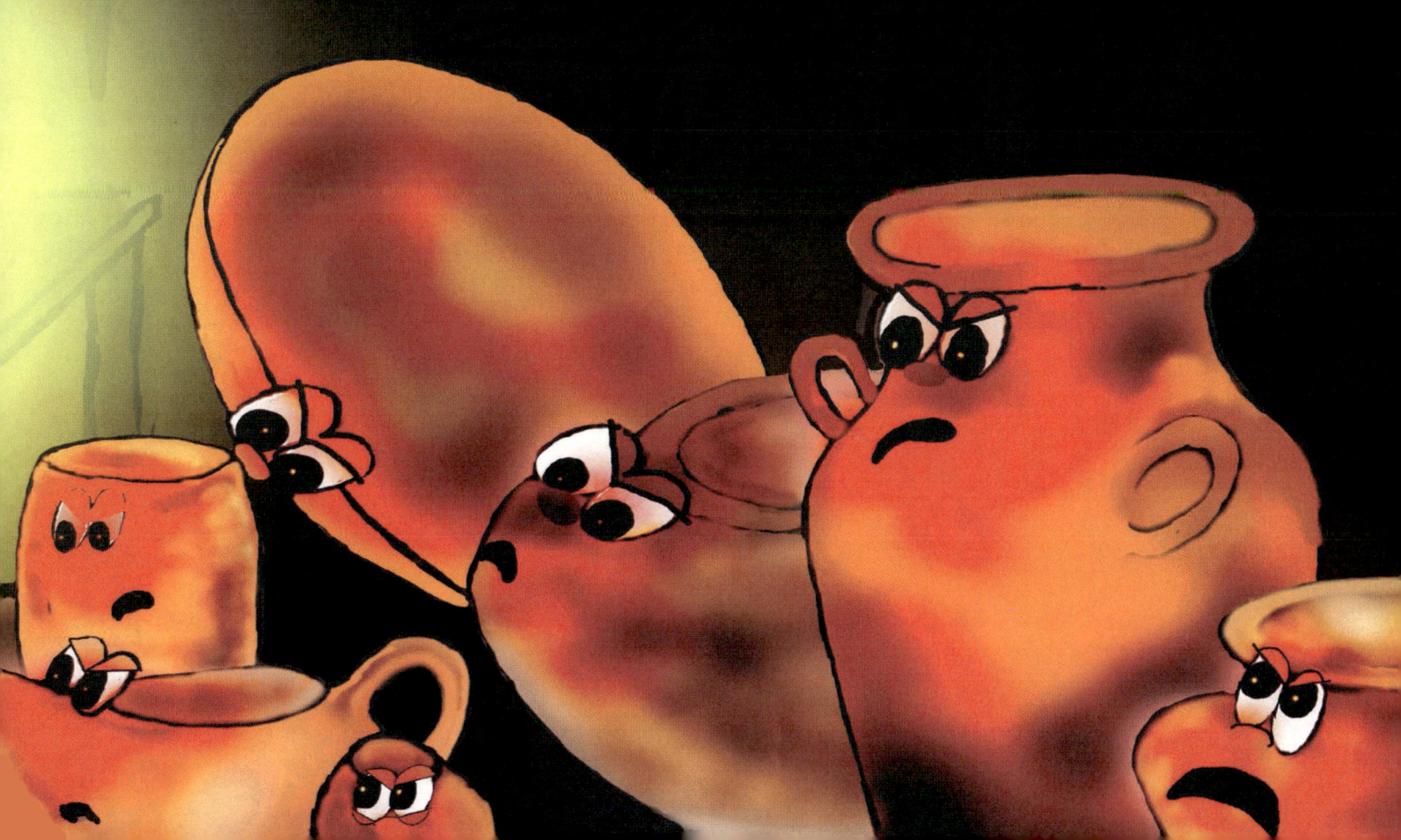

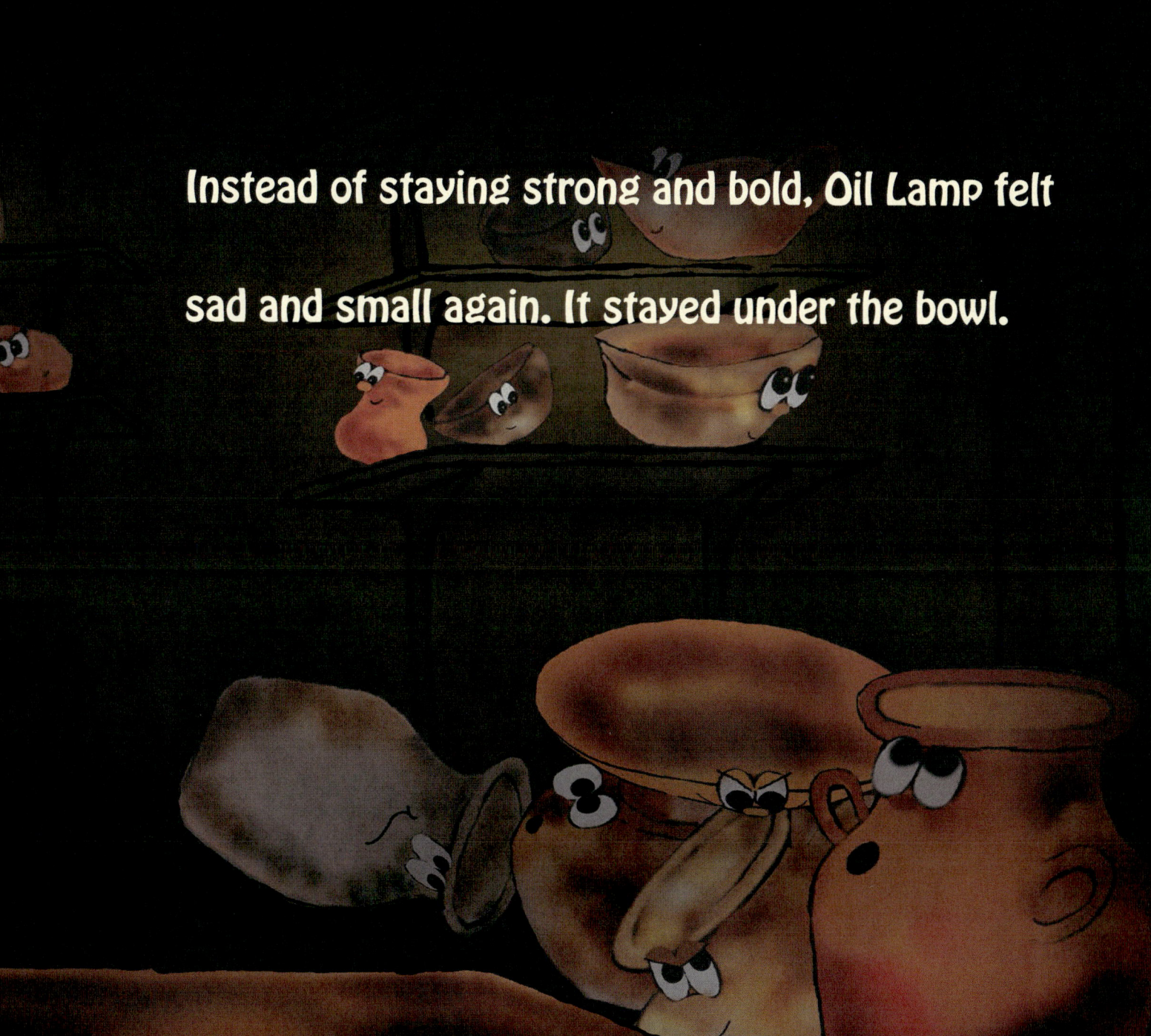

Instead of staying strong and bold, Oil Lamp felt sad and small again. It stayed under the bowl.

Little Pot and Tea Pot wanted Oil Lamp to understand that it could give light and warmth to the other vessels if only it stopped hiding under the bowl. They decided to share their stories.

"Before I became a fruit pot, I was scared and searched for a purpose, too," sprouted Little Pot. "Then I became selfish and tried to keep the fruit for myself."

"I was once too proud to lose my tea," whistled Tea Pot. "It stained my insides until the potter washed me clean."

"We learned that the potter makes our fruit and tea for sharing," said Little Pot. "The light you have brings good to others. Please come out and let it shine."

Oil Lamp listened and wanted to shine again, but it needed the potter and hoped he would come to light its flame.

Just then, the door opened. The potter came in and lit the wick. Oil Lamp smiled as the potter placed it high on a lampstand.

From atop the lampstand, Oil Lamp's light shone into all the corners of the workshop.

The other vessels slowly moved out of the shadows to bask in the light. Oil Lamp did not feel small or afraid anymore, and it did not burn too big or proud. Oil Lamp knew that its light had a purpose, and it was happy to let it shine.

A note from the author:

Our Potter wants each of us to shine lights. We do that by sharing Jesus with others. It takes bold faith and love to be light in a dark world. Just like Tea Pot and Little Pot, if we share our stories with others, they'll have courage to shine too. Keep shining!   - Dawn

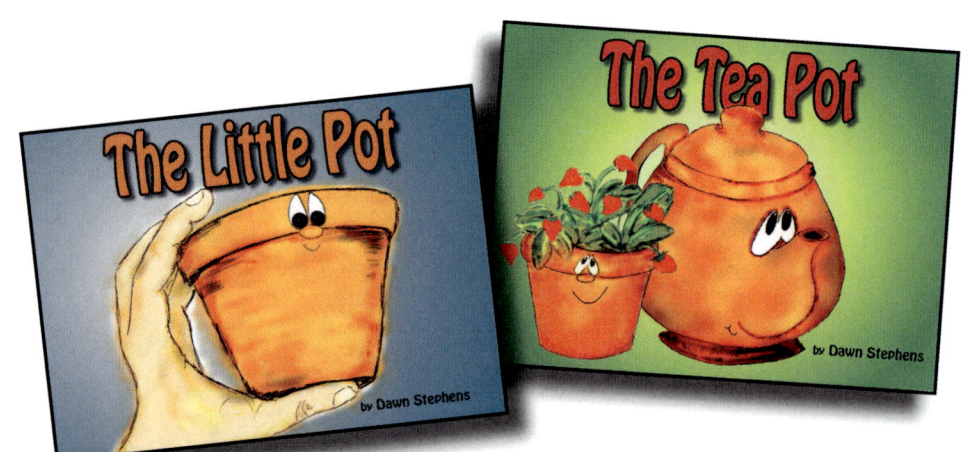

Check out other stories about Little Pot at
DawnStephensBooks.com

Made in the USA
Middletown, DE
19 September 2024